The Magical Animal

ADOPTION AGENCY

1 CLOVER'S LUCK

The Magical Animal

ADOPTION AGENCY

1 CLOVER'S LUCK

BY **Kallie George**

ILLUSTRATED BY

Alexandra Boiger

𝒟ısnɛʏ • HYPERION

LOS ANGELES NEW YORK

First Edition, February 2015
10 9 8 7 6 5 4 3 2 1
G475-5664-5-14319
Printed in the United States of America

Library of Congress Cataloging-in-Publication Data
George, Kallie.
Clover's luck / by Kallie George; illustrated by Alexandra Boiger.
—First edition.
pages cm.—(The Magical Animal Adoption Agency ; book 1)
Summary: Clover, who wants to change her bad luck, accepts a
volunteer position at a pet adoption agency unlike any other and soon
finds herself in a world of fairy horses, dragons with temperamental
snouts, wizards, princesses, and, unfortunately, witches.
ISBN 978-1-4231-8382-2—ISBN 1-4231-8382-7
[1. Imaginary creatures—Fiction. 2. Pet adoption—Fiction. 3. Magic—
Fiction. 4. Luck—Fiction.] I. Boiger, Alexandra, illustrator. II. Title.
PZ7.G293326Cl   2014
[Fic]—dc23   2013041940

Reinforced binding

Visit www.DisneyBooks.com

To my Nono, who knew I would be a writer
way before I did
—K.G.

To Vanessa and Andrea,
with love, always
—A.B.

Contents

1

Clover

Luck is like magic. It's mysterious and exciting and impossible to explain. It can't be described by equations or logic or even by books. You just have to believe.

Clover believed. She believed luck existed—and that all of hers was bad. From the time she was born under a moon as thin as a cat's whisker—a bad omen, she'd decided—her life had been filled with one misfortune after another, from burst bike tires to burnt toast. Not to mention problems with pets.

She tried everything to change her luck. She painted her room bright green, the color of lucky clover, her namesake, and pasted shooting stars on her ceiling that she could wish on every night. She hung a horseshoe over her bed and collected shiny pennies in a jar that she kept on her windowsill. She even carried a lucky charm with her at all times. This morning she had tucked a wishbone in her pocket. But nothing seemed to work.

The wishbone certainly wasn't helping her now. It was only the first day of vacation and already her whole summer had been ruined. Her best friend, Emma, had just called to tell her that she was going to Pony Camp after all. Both Emma and Clover had wanted to go, but the camp was full. This morning, though, someone had canceled, and Emma's name was first on the waiting list.

"Cheer up," Emma said when she gave Clover the news. "Maybe someone else will cancel, and you can come too."

But Clover knew that would never happen.

The camp lasted till school started. So much for sleepovers and sharing ice cream. So much for adventures and excitement. So much for spending the summer with her best friend.

"At least I have you," she said to Penny, her new pet

canary. "I can train you to sing and, well, do all sorts of things. It'll be fun."

Clover checked to make sure her bedroom window and door were tightly shut before taking Penny out of her cage. She was stroking the bird's yellow feathers when . . . *Smash!* A baseball broke through the window, narrowly missing the jar of pennies and a jade tortoise paperweight, and landed on her bed with a thump.

"Oh no!" Clover cried.

Quick as a wink, with just one tweet, Penny left Clover's finger and flew out through the hole left by the baseball.

"OH NO!" Clover cried even louder.

She ran out of her room, down the stairs, and out the front door. "Penny!" she shouted, racing after her bird, her shoes pounding the pavement. "Penny, come back!"

The street was empty. Whoever had thrown the ball was gone. Penny soared over the lawn and headed down the street. Clover chased after her.

At the end of the block, Penny perched on a picket fence. Clover tried to sneak up on the bird, but the moment she was within arm's reach, Penny took off, flying down the next block. Penny landed a few more times, but Clover still couldn't catch her.

Soon they reached the edge of the village. Penny kept on going. Clover had a stitch in her side, but she didn't stop either.

She ran through farmers' fields, over rolling hills, and along a twisty path that grew ever more rough and overgrown. She had never gone so far from the village. The stitch in her side grew into a knot.

The path took a turn, and she lost sight of Penny for a moment. When she rounded the bend, she froze. There before her was a line of trees and bushes, blocking her way like a great green wall. The Woods.

Her canary was perched atop a small, twisted tree, like a tiny star.

"Come to me, Penny! Good little bird," Clover called, holding out her finger. But as she crept closer, Penny gave a cheeky tweet and flew off, disappearing into the Woods.

Keep away, keep away, the Woods are where wee beasties play. The rhyme sung at school echoed in Clover's

head. People from her village stayed far away from the Woods. They were a strange place, and even stranger lands lay beyond them—or so the rumors rang.

The trees ahead creaked and groaned, and shadows flickered. An eerie breeze whistled through the branches as if in tune to the rhyme.

Clover gulped and reached for the wishbone in her pocket. So far it hadn't proved lucky, but she would give it one more chance.

She took a deep breath and looked for a path. There was a tiny trail so overgrown it was hard to see, but when she pushed past the first few bushes, it opened up.

The trees cast dark shadows, but were also lush and green. Rotting logs covered the forest floor, yet so did feathery moss, dotted with white flowers. The air smelled clean and fresh.

The Woods were beautiful, and only slightly ominous. They weren't strange at all. But Penny was nowhere to be seen. She was gone. Really gone.

"Stupid bad luck!" Clover said, blinking back tears. She reached into her pocket again and pulled out the wishbone. "This is the worst charm yet!" She threw it away as hard as she could.

The wishbone glanced off a stump, bounced back, and almost hit her in the face.

But Clover didn't notice. She was staring at a large sheet of thick yellow paper nailed to the trunk of a nearby tree. The paper was curled and faded, the hand-written message streaked from rain.

Clover stepped closer to read it.

DO YOU LOVE ANIMALS?
DO YOU WANT TO HELP THEM
FIND HAPPY HOMES?
OUR AGENCY NEEDS YOU!
VOLUNTEER AT THE M.A.A.A.

At the bottom were little slips of paper with directions. Not one had been torn off.

Clover read the notice again. And then a third time. She desperately wanted a pet of her own. But Penny's escape made it clear—once and for all—that she was just too unlucky.

If I worked at an animal adoption agency, she thought, *I could be with animals without actually owning a pet. I could help them. I could set things right.*

Carefully, she tore off the first slip and read it.

"The M.A.A.A.—#1 Dragon's Tail Lane. Down the path. Just around the bend. Follow the signs."

She hesitated for a moment. Going into the Woods to chase her bird was one thing. Going to apply for a volunteer position was quite another. Who would run an animal adoption agency in the Woods? Weren't beasties supposed to be the only creatures that lived here?

Clover looked around again. The treetops bobbed in the wind. A squirrel chattered to its friend. Already there were creatures other than beasties.

Just around the bend, thought Clover. *That's not too far to go. I can at least check it out.*

Folding the slip in two, she stuck it deep in her pocket and set off down the path, in search of the first sign. Despite her unluckiness, Clover always kept a hopeful heart.

2

The Agency

Signs were scarce, and it took Clover much longer than she expected to wind her way through the Woods.

At one point she reached a place where the path branched in many directions. Nailed onto a huge tree in the center were several signs shaped like arrows. SHOPPES made sense. Though she was surprised to find there were shops in the Woods. What kinds of shops would they be? Not ordinary ones that sold shoes or sweets, surely. But if there was an adoption agency, who knew?

MEADOWS and OUT also made sense. The OUT sign pointed to the path that she was standing on, so it must mean out of the Woods and to her village.

But HEART and BEYOND were a little more puzzling. The HEART sign pointed down a dark, twisty path. *Maybe it leads into the heart of the Woods,* thought Clover. So, did BEYOND mean there were villages and towns on the other side of the Woods? She looked to see what kind of path it pointed to and nearly tripped on an arrow lying flat on the ground.

She picked it up. M.A.A.A. was etched into the wood in black letters.

"Oh no," Clover moaned. "Now how will I find it?"

She looked again at the other arrows. All the paths except the one to the far left were clearly marked.

Was that the path to the Agency? It had to be.

Leaning the arrow against the tree, she started down the path to the left. It wasn't long before she came to a clearing, and she could see what appeared to be a charming cottage in the distance, with smoke curling out from a chimney. Where the path narrowed, there was a sign that read DRAGON'S TAIL LANE. There wasn't really a lane to speak of, not like at home, but there were no other buildings in sight, so that had to be it. A sense of well-being filled her. She felt almost . . . lucky.

But that feeling lasted only a moment. Dark clouds had filled the sky, and it began to rain. Hard. Soon raindrops dripped from her nose.

To top it off, a lady clutching a white kitten bustled by and bumped into her. Clover stepped out of the way and right into a mud puddle.

Dressed in a billowing black raincoat, her face hidden by the floppy brim of her hat, the lady looked like a thundercloud. The kitten, unprotected and dripping, mewed as they passed.

"Mind your way," snapped the lady, as though it were Clover's fault.

Mind your kitten, Clover wanted to reply, but the words caught in her throat as the lady hurried away.

Clover thought things couldn't get worse.

But, of course, they could. And they did.

The Agency was tucked away at the end of the path, which curved like a giant tail. Whether it was like a dragon's tail, as the sign said, Clover wasn't sure. The only dragons she had seen were those in storybooks.

This Agency too seemed like it had popped out of the pages of a storybook.

Number 1 Dragon's Tail Lane was a large, low-lying wooden building with a thatched roof covered in moss as thick as fur. Vines snaked up its sides, and a thin tendril of smoke rose out of a chimney at the back. Protruding from the right was a rickety tower. An old wooden fence circled the building like a toothy grin. At the front gate stood a small, sleepy-looking garden gnome. Over the gate a sign read:

WELCOME TO THE M.A.A.A

The bottom of the last letter *A* was partly missing, and ragged, as though something had bitten it off. Something big.

It didn't scare her exactly, but it *was* startling. Clover felt in her pocket, forgetting for a moment that she

had thrown her wishbone away, and touched the slip of paper she had torn off the sign instead. Her heart took courage.

Feet squishing in her shoes, she trudged through the gate, up the path, and up the steps. An ENTER sign hung on the doorknob, but underneath, in tiny letters, were the words AT YOUR OWN RISK. This sign looked eaten too—nibbled around the edges. The doorknob was made from wood, carved in the shape of a beak.

Slowly, she pushed open the door.

The room smelled faintly of smoke and looked as if it hadn't been cleaned in years; everything was dusty and old. There was a tilting bookshelf brimming with books and a desk piled high with papers. A red quill pen stuck out of a bottle of ink. A small silver bell perched on a stack of papers on the desk with a sign reading RING FOR SERVICE.

Beside the desk, on a thick rug, were two chairs and a couch around a small coffee table. On the table were pamphlets titled *From Spark to Flame: How to Encourage Friendly Fires*; *Proper Care of Unusual Eggs*; and *Troublesome Toads: When Warts Turn Weird*.

An enormous golden book rested on a stand, in a corner by itself.

Although the room was cluttered, there were no pictures or posters of cute little animals on the walls like Clover was used to seeing at every pet shop and vet's office she had ever been in, only a slogan on a hook behind the desk: NO ANIMAL IS TOO UNUSUAL TO ADOPT. Clover liked that. Perhaps this agency dealt with pets like parrots and hedgehogs.

She rang the bell, being careful not to knock over the papers.

She waited for a long time, but there was no response.

She was about to leave when a door behind the desk burst open and out came an old man.

"Wait a minute. Don't be so impatient," he called, as though he was annoyed at being disturbed.

He was only a tad taller than Clover, with a short, pointed white beard. His shirt was streaked with soot.

He examined Clover with raised eyebrows, from her mud-splattered stockings and dress to the water dripping off her freckled nose.

"May I help you?" he asked.

"Excuse me, is this the Animal Adoption Agency? This is my first time in the Woods. I lost my bird and found you instead."

The old man's bushy eyebrows rose higher. "I'm

sorry," he said after a pause, "but we can't help you here. Lost birds are a lost cause; but if it is in the Woods, it will surely make friends."

"Oh," said Clover. "I hope you're right. But that's not why I'm here. I came to volunteer."

The man looked her up and down again intently, then shook his head. "You're out of luck."

"I always am."

"I didn't mean—" the man began, seeing how upset she was, but Clover kept talking.

"I'm especially unlucky with pets. My fish jumped out of his cup and went down the drain when I was cleaning his bowl. My mom was allergic to my puppy, and we had to give her away. My kitten decided he liked our neighbor's house better than ours and stayed there. And now my bird . . ." Clover gulped.

"I highly doubt—" The man tried to jump in again, but Clover still didn't stop.

"My parents like me to have a pet, because they're so busy working and don't want me to be lonely. Plus they know I love animals. But I'm too unlucky to keep a pet myself. Maybe I can help out here instead. I saw your notice on a tree." Clover showed him the slip of paper.

The man tugged at his beard with one hand and tapped on the desk with his other.

Clover slumped. "I'll . . . I'll go now."

"Wait," he said. "What animals are you afraid of?"

She gave him a puzzled look. "None. Not even big ones. I went to the zoo once in the city, and I saw an enormous elephant and two huge lions. I wasn't scared at all. In fact, I felt sorry for them. They looked so unhappy."

"Can you help every day?"

"Yes, I can."

"But what about school?"

"It's summer. There's no school."

He nodded. "Ah, of course. Good." He leaned closer, resting his elbows on the desk and looking straight into Clover's eyes. "Now for the most important question. You must answer honestly. Can you keep a secret?"

"Yes," she replied, slowly but without hesitation. "I don't really have many people to tell things to anyway." This was especially true now that Emma was gone.

The man nodded. "Then I've changed my mind. You may have bad luck with regular pets, but you might fit in perfectly here."

"What do you mean?"

"My name is Mr. Jams, and this"—the old man paused and gestured to the room—"this is the M.A.A.A.: the Magical Animal Adoption Agency."

"Magical animals?" Clover's eyes grew wide.

Mr. Jams pulled out his pocket watch. "Oh, cripes and clawscratch! I don't have time to explain right now. I have a lot to do today. Be back here at seven o'clock sharp tomorrow, and I'll begin your training."

"Tomorrow morning?"

"Of course, and don't be late," said Mr. Jams sternly. With that, he turned, pulled open the door behind the desk, and disappeared.

The small sign on the wall shook as the door slammed shut. Clover reread the words on it:

This time, they made her tingle.

3

The Small Animals

By the time Clover got home, it was already late afternoon. Her parents were still at work at the mayor's office, as usual. Clover didn't really mind. She was used to it. She had everything she needed, including a number for emergencies, and her parents always checked in to make sure she was okay.

Besides, being alone meant that it was easy to keep secrets. It also gave her plenty of time to ponder things, like what Mr. Jams meant about the magical animals.

She thought about it as she cleaned up her room and taped cardboard over her broken window. She thought about it as she warmed up the supper her parents had left for her in the fridge. (It was her favorite, macaroni and cheese.)

She was so distracted thinking about magical animals that she dropped and broke not just her glass but also her plate when she was doing the dishes. And at bedtime, her toothbrush slipped into the soap dish, and no matter how much she rinsed it, it still tasted like soap.

Even so, she couldn't stop wondering what Mr. Jams had meant.

They must be pets for magicians, she finally decided. She liked that. Maybe magicians' pets had their own built-in luck.

When Clover's mom called just before bedtime, Clover told her about Penny but not about the Agency. Her mom listened sympathetically and afterward, encouraged by the conversation, Clover sketched a picture of her lost bird. It took a mix of her gold and orange colored pencils to get the color right. When she was done, she pinned it onto her Memory Wall, next to the pictures of her fish and her puppy.

From the time she was tiny, Clover had loved animals. Her first word hadn't been "Mama" or "Papa";

about you." Mr. Jams strode through the door behind the desk, turned, and, with a wave of his hand, beckoned Clover to follow. "This way."

Mr. Jams kept munching his toast as they passed a storage room filled with boxes. A rope ladder hung down from the ceiling like a swing. There were cages too—some with bent bars, and one that looked like it had been melted. *I wonder if there was a fire here*, Clover thought. Before she could take a closer look, Mr. Jams continued down the hall.

They passed more rooms: a laundry room, a washing room with tubs of various sizes that hung from the ceiling like strange decorations, and a kitchen that contained the biggest refrigerator she had ever seen, with three separate doors. In one corner sat a giant black cauldron. She didn't know cauldrons like that really existed.

Halfway down the hall, Mr. Jams pointed to the right. "This way leads to my quarters." He pointed to the left. "That way leads to the room where we keep the smaller animals. Straight ahead leads to the stables, where the bigger pens and stalls are."

A muffled roar came from that direction. Clover jumped. So did Mr. Jams.

"Cripes and clawscratch! Snort must be in trouble again. Acquaint yourself with our smaller pets. I'll be back momentarily."

Mr. Jams hurried out, gulping down the last bit of his toast as he went.

With a knot in her stomach, Clover opened the door and stepped into a big room lined with small cages and tanks. It was warm and smelled like the forest.

In the first tank was a tiny pool of water surrounded by moss. Nestled in the moss was a glass ball, and sitting on top of the ball was what Clover thought at first was another lump of moss. But the card on the bottom corner of the tank said it was a toad named Esmeralda.

Clover was disappointed. She had been expecting magicians' pets like cute white bunnies, not a warty green toad.

But then she read the rest of the card and gasped.

HISTORY: This toad was discovered long ago in a well, abandoned and under a curse. Unfortunately we could not lift the curse, but its effects appear to be benign. Our oldest resident, Esmeralda would make the perfect companion for a patient, color-loving client.

26

A curse? What does that mean? Clover looked back into the tank and, to her amazement, Esmeralda's warts had changed color. Instead of green they were now a startling orange!

"Oh!" Clover pressed her face against the glass. Suddenly, Esmeralda snapped out her tongue, hitting the glass right above Clover's eyes.

She jumped back in surprise. The toad seemed to glare at her.

"I'm sorry," said Clover. "I didn't mean to upset you." The toad let out a loud croak, then hopped into the water with a splash.

Cautiously, Clover turned to the tank that came next.

It was quite a bit larger than the toad's tank, and decorated like a miniature forest, with ferns and moss and sticks and a few lumps of what seemed to be white sugar. Clover looked closely, but she couldn't see anything else. Then out from the ferns paraded five tiny horses—the smallest, prettiest horses she had ever seen. They were all shades of gray and white with tails no longer than her little finger, and hooves no bigger than her fingernails. Two jumped over the sticks, which to them were as big as logs, while the others settled in to lick the sugar cubes.

"Miniature horses!" she cried. "They're so cute!"
She read the card.

NAMES: Acorn, Hickory, Tansy, Butternut &
Buttercup
SPECIES: Fairy Horses
AGE: 200 years
HISTORY: These gentle horses were rescued from
a cave where they were being held captive and
mistreated by ogres. They are workhorses by

nature, and with consistent good treatment
would happily plow a fairy's field or pull a
small wagon filled with peas or flowers.

A shiver of excitement ran through Clover's body.
What else might she find? She turned quickly to see the
next animals.

In a large tank, a big black rock rose up to form
a peak like a small volcano. Lounging on one side of
the rock, like thin sticks of red licorice, were two salamanders. They were unlike any salamanders Clover
had ever seen. Steam rose from their nostrils. Clover
touched her fingertips lightly to the glass. It was hot.

The card said:

NAMES: Ash and Flame
SPECIES: Elemental Salamanders, commonly
known as Fire Salamanders
AGE: Indeterminate, considered immortal
HISTORY: The previous owner gave these
salamanders up because she feared the long-
term commitment of an immortal pet. They
are perfect adoptees for a family with a
constantly heated hearth.

Clover turned to the next cage. It was empty. She took a deep breath. She was trembling. *These aren't magicians' pets at all. They must be the pets of the strange people that live in the Woods and Beyond.* She had always imagined that the creatures that lived in the Woods were scary—after all, they *were* called "beasties." But so far this hadn't been the case. *These* animals certainly weren't scary beasties. They were *magical*. Really, truly magical.

Although she believed in luck and charms, she had never believed *this* kind of magic existed. She wished her best friend were around. Emma would love this. She was always talking about the magic creatures found in her storybooks as if they were real.

And now it turned out that they were.

4

The
Stables

"That used to house a grimalkin, a witch's kitten." Mr. Jams's voice startled Clover. He was standing beside her now, pointing to the empty cage.

"Witches' cats are usually black, but that fellow was white. I found him in a ditch in the Woods. Some cranky witch must have culled him out of a black cat's litter, or maybe the mother herself abandoned him. Anyway, he was adopted right before you arrived yesterday, and the witch who adopted him seemed particularly pleased that he was white. A bit of an unusual case. But enough of that," he said. "It's time for you to meet the other animals. Come on. Don't just stand there tongue-tied like a troll." He chuckled.

Clover followed Mr. Jams out of the room for small animals and down the hall that he had told her led to the stables.

He pointed to a closed door on the right. "In there we have an aviary for phoenixes and other magical birds, but we haven't had any of those for a long time. And through that door," he said, gesturing to the one beside it, "are large tanks, in case we get abandoned sea serpents or hippocampi."

He noticed Clover's puzzled expression and explained, "Hippocampi are sea horses. Not the tiny sea horses you may be familiar with, but actual sea *horses*. Horse from the waist up and fish from the waist down. They eat only sea foam. It takes hours to froth up salty water, so be thankful we don't have one right now."

They passed several other rooms with closed doors and soon reached the end of the hall. "Through here are our stables, where we keep our unicorns. You know what those are, I assume?"

Clover nodded promptly, and held her breath as they walked into the stables. Soft whinnies and the sound of swishing tails greeted her, along with the smell of hay and, strangely, smoke. It was a giant barn with large stalls in two rows facing each other.

The stalls on the left housed unicorns more beautiful than any picture in Emma's books. They poked their heads up over the gates, their long horns raised toward her. Their manes and horns were as white as milk. A few looked directly at her with their blue eyes. The unicorns were much smaller than Clover imagined unicorns would be—hardly as tall as she. The smallest one, closest to the door, came up to her shoulder.

Clover could barely believe that only a day ago she had been jealous of Emma going to Pony Camp, and now here she was, face-to-face with honest-to-goodness unicorns.

"We always have a lot of unicorns," said Mr. Jams. "At the moment there are half a dozen. That is a manageable herd. But at times we have had as many as a dozen. Unicorns are popular gifts for young princesses, and, well, spoiled princesses

34

get a unicorn whenever they demand one. All too often they become bored with their new pet and abandon it or give it to us. But unicorns are easy to look after. Water and mush is all they need. They're shy, and the ones we get here often feel unloved. They need a gentle touch. That little one came to us only a few days ago," said Mr. Jams. "But he is very sweet. Hold out your hand. And mind his horn."

Clover did. Gingerly the little creature nuzzled her fingers. His nose was soft, dry, and cool.

She could see how thin he was. Every rib was visible. His tail was so long it dusted the ground, and his forelock fell over his eyes. But saddest-looking of all was his horn, which was rounded and short, as though it had never properly grown.

"Poor thing," murmured Clover, picking up a handful of hay from a barrel beside the stall and holding it out. The unicorn quickly ate it up. Clover glanced at the card on the stall gate.

"Mistypoo Moondrop," she read aloud. "Mistypoo? Is that really his name?"

"That's a princess for you," Mr. Jams said with a grunt. "Less sense than a sprite. This fellow's history is especially unfortunate. The princess not only gave him that name, she didn't care for him at all and didn't feed him properly. She filed down his horn because she thought a rounded horn was more stylish. I call him Moondrop and never use his first name. Unlike most unicorns, he wasn't abandoned. Another princess told me about the situation and I investigated, and then I seized him."

"But if princesses abandon unicorns, who adopts them?"

"Usually other princesses," said Mr. Jams with a sigh. "Hopefully they are good, compassionate princesses, ones who really *want* unicorns."

"That's a lot of princesses!" exclaimed Clover.

"Well, there are a lot of little kingdoms beyond the Woods. Too bad most of the kings and queens aren't better parents. I have a drawer full of special paperwork for princesses. I'll show you later. At least these creatures are better off than Snort. Who knows *who* will adopt him. . . ."

"Who is Snort?"

"Stay close and I'll show you."

Clover left Moondrop to follow Mr. Jams. On the left, they passed more unicorns, with cards pinned to their stall gates. There wasn't time to read them now, but she wondered what their names were and planned to go back and check as soon as she could. On the right,

36

after the tack room, which Mr. Jams mumbled was for "saddles and such," and a room for storing straw and hay, there were giant pens, much bigger and completely enclosed. Each had a square window to let in light. All were empty. "For a while a griffin lived in this one," Mr. Jams said. He pointed to another pen. "And a winged horse lived in that one."

"A winged horse?" Clover repeated, in amazement.

"Similar to a unicorn, but bigger, and with wings instead of a horn," explained Mr. Jams.

"I know. I mean, I didn't *know* know, but . . . Oh!" exclaimed Clover as she looked up. They had finally reached the very back corner, where the biggest pen stood. It was three times larger than any of the others and was made entirely of bricks. Buckets filled with water surrounded it, and they had to climb over them to get to the metal door.

"Have a look," instructed Mr. Jams, gesturing to a small glassless window. Clover inched forward and peered in.

No hay was strewn on the floor of this pen. The only thing inside was the creature living there.

"A dragon!" she gasped.

Indeed it was a small, but not tiny, dragon. He lay curled up in a ball in the middle of the floor, looking somewhat like the remains of a campfire, an ashy black heap. His tail ended in a heart-shaped point, and his wings, pressed to his sides, looked like black paper fans. From large nostrils, wisps of smoke curled up toward the ceiling. The dragon raised his head briefly, and, seeing Clover and Mr. Jams were there, jumped up, stood on his hind feet, and thumped his tail on the ground.

"There, there, Snort," said Mr. Jams through the window. "Calm down, you fiery fellow."

Snort stopped thumping his tail and dropped down to all fours. His eyes were green like emeralds, and his nostrils were as big as Clover's fist.

"Snort's just a baby. Every time he sneezes or coughs, or simply becomes overly excited, he snorts flames. I am not sure who abandoned him here. I found him tied to a post by the gate one morning. I assume that his fire problem is why. Even though there's nothing in his pen to catch on fire, I keep the buckets of water close by, just in case. And there's a chimney in the ceiling to let out the smoke. Several knights have come by wanting to adopt him, but I turned them away." Mr. Jams sighed. "Now, that's not to say I don't want a good home for Snort. But

knights, as you probably know, like to slay dragons. No prize is greater to a knight than a dragon-head trophy."

A dark and far-off look came over Mr. Jams. He turned to Clover. "Many people want magical animals, but not all of them for the right reasons. Our creatures are meant for those who truly deserve them, those with good hearts. The animals at our Agency aren't possessions to be shown off, but companions, pets to be loved and cared for. This is something that even residents of the Woods and lands Beyond have trouble understanding, so we can't expect people unfamiliar with magic to understand either, which is why word of the Agency cannot spread outside the Woods. You must keep the Agency secret from everyone, even your parents and friends, and you must carefully check each customer who comes in."

Clover knew it would be tough, especially not to tell Emma when she returned, but she knew how important it was. She looked Mr. Jams straight in the eye. "I will. I promise," she said.

"But take heart," said Mr. Jams. "In general, you will find the people of the Woods are a good sort."

"What about the beasties?" Clover couldn't help but burst out.

"Beasties?"

"You know, like in the rhyme: *Keep away, keep away, the Woods are where wee beasties play.*"

Mr. Jams chuckled. "Ah, yes. I think it was Lester the leprechaun who made that up. Non-magic folk are quick to believe in rumors. Although we have our share of bad princesses and knights and even wicked witches, there are no beasties," Mr. Jams assured her. "And, in fact, there were no Woods either until we put them here. The Woods were created long ago as a boundary between your world and the magic one. The magic folk prefer to keep to themselves and perpetuate the myth of beasties and other scary things to keep humans out. Humans are curious, but very few are willing to risk crossing the boundary. Over time the Woods have been populated by a few people and creatures who don't quite fit in anywhere else."

"What about me?" Clover asked. "I don't really belong here."

Mr. Jams simply winked.

Clover was about to ask him again, unsure if he had heard her, when he gestured to Snort.

"The trick is to make sure he's nice and calm before you feed him. He looks calm now," said Mr. Jams. "Why don't you introduce yourself?" He opened the door.

Clover took tentative steps into the pen, with Mr.

Jams behind her. Snort didn't budge. She reached out her hand.

"Can you see how his tail is thumping? He likes you," said Mr. Jams.

"He does?" whispered Clover. "I like him too."

"Ah, a gentle heart you have, my dear. But beware. Although I have mentioned the many characters I refuse to let adopt our animals, there are far more for whom I've arranged adoptions. Adoption is our Agency's purpose. It can be hard to part ways with our animals, but the Agency isn't a home for them. You will need to guard your heart, even as you keep it open."

Clover understood. At least, she thought she did.

"I do hope someone adopts Snort soon," added Mr. Jams. "Although his wings are small now, they are growing quickly. Then we'll have new problems to deal with."

"Will he start flying?" asked Clover, looking at his delicate wings. They seemed so thin and frail, all folded up on his back. It was hard to imagine them lifting him into the air.

"Yes, though pet dragons don't fly much. Their wings never grow too big. *Wild* dragons are a different matter. Their wings can grow to the length of these stables when spread out fully. Go ahead," continued Mr. Jams. "Give his scales a scratch. He likes it."

She was just about to when . . .

Just her luck. A piece of hay from feeding Moondrop had stuck to her sleeve and now it came loose—right as Snort took in a deep breath. He inhaled it.

His nostrils flared.

"Oh no!" cried Clover. "Duck!"

She and Mr. Jams threw themselves onto the ground.

A giant flame burst out of Snort's nostrils and whizzed over their heads, scorching the brick wall above the door.

"Holy buckets, that was close," Mr. Jams said as they cautiously stood up and backed out. Mr. Jams closed the door and latched it.

"I told you I was unlucky," said Clover apologetically.

"It has nothing to do with you. Snort is a fire hazard. That's all there is to it. You were as quick as a pixie. That's just the kind of instincts a good volunteer needs."

But Clover wasn't so sure.

"Now, let's get to work," said Mr. Jams. "I have a lot more to show you."

Clover nodded. Before following Mr. Jams, she glanced back at Snort through the window.

He was curled up in a ball again, with his tail covering his snout. Clover understood how he felt.

It wasn't fun to be unable to control what you did. Not one bit.

5

The
Note

At the end of the first day, Mr. Jams swore her to secrecy *again*. When she got home, she was surprised to find both her parents there, and she was immediately tempted to break the promise. After all, so much had happened. But she didn't. Instead, at supper, when they asked about her day, she told them she was volunteering at an animal adoption agency and it was fun, and nothing more. Not a lie, but not the full truth either.

"Oh, Clover, that's wonderful. We're so proud of you," her mom said. "See, if you're plucky, you'll be lucky. Good things *do* happen to you. Clover *is* a lucky name."

"But what about . . ." started Clover, but then paused. There were so many things she could list.

"I know," said her mom softly. "Penny, right? Poor Penny. Are you okay?"

"Yes. I have the Agency's pets to play with now," said Clover, thinking, *Dragons and unicorns and fairy horses,* but she didn't say this aloud. She doubted they would believe her even if she did.

"So you do," said her dad. "Why, I remember my first job. My sister and I had a lemonade stand—I was in charge of all our signs and posters."

"I had to design a poster today at work," said her mom, "and pamphlets too. . . ."

And so began another supper talking about work. Clover was grateful that her parents didn't ask any other questions about the Agency. It was one good thing about having parents obsessed with their work. And now she wondered if maybe she had inherited their trait, since all she could think about was work too. Although the Agency wasn't really work. It was too much fun.

That night, instead of magicians' pets, Clover dreamed of the amazing animals she had seen at the Agency—the toad and the fairy horses, the salamanders and the unicorns, and the dragon. She even dreamed of the little white kitten.

She dreamed of all the things she had done with Mr. Jams—feeding and cleaning, and sorting the papers.

And in her dream, everyone, even the animals, ate cinnamon toast.

♣

The next morning, Clover woke up right as the sun was rising. With a sandwich in one pocket and a bunch of fresh carrots for Moondrop in the other, she headed to the Agency. She soon realized she was walking with a bounce in her step. Immediately she corrected this. There was no point getting too happy. Something was bound to go wrong.

And indeed, when she reached the Agency door, it was locked. The ENTER sign was turned to CLOSED (EVEN FOR ROYALTY!). The garden gnome, which she'd previously seen by the gate, was now standing beside the door. Under his foot was an envelope.

She pulled it out. On the front, in swirly handwriting, was her name:

Quickly, she tore it open.

Dear Clover,

I have been called away on an extremely important rescue mission. I would usually have my cousin look after the Agency, but he's unavailable. Luckily, there's you. I hate to leave you on your own so soon, but I have every confidence that you will be able to look after the Agency in my absence.

I will return the day after tomorrow. There are plenty of supplies.

I forgot to mention to you that Esmeralda the toad needs a vitamin pill every day. Curses can be very draining. The pills are kept in a large purple bottle on the shelf under her tank. Also, Coco the unicorn is allergic to sugar beets. Make sure she doesn't come in contact with the sugar beet biscuits.

In all other matters, simply do as I showed you yesterday. There is a copy of the feeding schedule in the kitchen cupboard beside the cauldron. I've cleaned all the cages and stables, but you will need to change the hay in the unicorns' stables every day. Snort burns up all his messes. The adoption papers are in the third drawer. They should be easy to understand. Just make sure that all the boxes are filled in. You can help yourself to tea and cinnamon toast.

Please find the key inside this envelope.

Lock up when it is time for you to go home. The gnome will guard the Agency at night. He sleeps during the day.

The animals are counting on you.

—Mr. Jams

P.S.—Remember: be wary of princesses, knights, and witches; they can be both good and bad.
P.P.S.—If an animal falls ill, phone Dr. Nurtch. She's a magical-animal vet. The number is in the jam jar on the desk.

Clover's heart sank. She shook her head. *I can't look after the Agency all by myself.*

She looked down at the garden gnome. His eyes, open before, were now closed. If Clover hadn't just seen it, she would never have thought he was alive. He looked just like one of the clay gnomes in her neighbor's yard. She wondered briefly if they were alive too.

There was no one else around.

"The animals are probably hungry for their breakfasts, right?" she asked him.

He didn't answer.

"Why can't you just look after them?"

At this the gnome's eyes blinked open. He stared at her hard.

She gulped. "I guess you would be too tired, looking after the Agency all night and then all day too?"

The gnome said nothing.

"But I only just came here. I barely know anything. And plus, Mr. Jams knows I'm unlucky! I told him."

The gnome seemed to stare at her harder.

She thought of all the animals inside. Skinny Moondrop, Snort with his fire problem, Esmeralda and her curse. Being unlucky was something she shared with them. They were worse off, really, because they needed looking after. And she was the only one there, the only one who could.

She took a deep breath. "Well, it *is* only for two days," she said. "Maybe everything will be okay."

51

The gnome's clay mustache rose up in a smile.

It made Clover feel good. "Two days. I can do it."

She looked back at the gnome. But his eyes were shut again, and when she leaned close to him she thought she heard a faint grunting, like snoring. He was already asleep.

Clover took the key from the envelope. It was really fancy with sharp, pointy teeth and, upon closer examination, looked as if it had been carved from an animal's tooth. Probably a magical animal's, thought Clover, though it looked too small to be a dragon's. After opening the front door and letting herself in, she used the string from the bunch of carrots to tie the key around her wrist. After all, it would be just her luck to lose it.

Then she hurried to the back to greet the animals and begin the day.

Of course, it wasn't easy.

Even though she had paid close attention yesterday,

there was lots to remember. Thank goodness Mr. Jams was well organized.

Each of the doors of the refrigerator was labeled. The biggest door read LARGE MEALS, the medium-sized door SNACKS, and the smallest door MISCELLANEOUS. She opened the biggest door to find the dragon's food, already portioned out in bags. Behind the snacks door were big bags of rosy apples and small ones of baby bean sprouts. There was a jar of squashed flies in there too, for Esmeralda, with a pair of tweezers inside and a note that said, *Maximum fourteen a day.*

Behind the miscellaneous door was food Mr. Jams hadn't explained to her. A bag that said "Slew Guts," a jar of "Friggles," and a box of "Panadalls." *I wonder what kinds of animals eat these,* thought Clover.

In the big cupboard were the special oats to make mush to feed the unicorns and the fairy horses. There was a label on each colorful bin saying how many scoops to mix together with water. The fairy horses only took one pellet of each, dry, and there was a tin of sugar cubes for them too. The small cupboard was full of jars of jam and honey, cinnamon and sugar, a loaf of bread, and a box of tea. These were clearly for Mr. Jams.

Of course, the one food Clover couldn't find was the salamanders'. And of all the foods to forget, this was the worst, because Mr. Jams said they absolutely HAD to eat first thing in the morning because they burned up a lot of energy.

Just my luck, she thought. Then she took a deep breath and tried to think logically. They were fire salamanders, so maybe they needed spicy food, like hot sauce or hot peppers. Her mom kept their hot peppers hanging up in their pantry, where it was cool and dark. Clover checked the back of the kitchen. There, on a shelf, was a row of jars of crushed peppers, with gloves hanging from a peg. *Fire Salamander food—one pepper each. Extra spicy. Use the gloves.*

"Hellooo!" said the princess again upon seeing Clover, and added, with a note of surprise in her voice, "Who are *you*? Where's that dotty old man?"

"I'm new here," said Clover, not wanting to tell her that she had just started the day before. "What can I help you with?"

"Well, my dear, first of all, you can help me by addressing me as 'Your Highness.' I am a royal princess, as you can well see." She took a step closer to the desk, and Clover swore she smelled like onions and garlic.

Strange. I imagined princesses would smell like roses and strawberries. Of course, Clover didn't say this out loud.

"And then you shall serve me, my dear, by showing me the unicorns you have for adoption. I am looking for a sweet, darling unicorn to love and look after, forever and always. I am just dyyyying for one. I've been waiting a loooong time. I am shy, just like unicorns are, and it has taken me aaaages to get up the courage to come here and get one. So, my dear, be a good little servant and show them to me."

Clover remembered Mr. Jams's warning about princesses. "One moment, please," she said, and searched through the cabinet's drawers until she found the form titled Precautions for Princess Adoptions Regarding Unicorns.

The three starred items on the list, the requirements all princesses must meet, caught her eye.

★1 Determine the reason the princess wants a pet: a long-term companion or a birthday surprise? Unicorns are not to be adopted as gifts.

★2 Determine the princess's age. Older princesses are usually more reliable than young ones.

★3 Observe the princess with a unicorn. She MUST be kind and gentle when petting it.

Well, this princess met two of the requirements. She was certainly old, and she said she wanted a unicorn not for a birthday present, but to love forever. She was definitely bossy, but Clover had never met a princess before. Likely they all acted that way.

"We do have unicorns," Clover said at last, adding quickly, "Your Highness. We have lots of them. Follow me."

Clover led the princess through the door and down the hall. The princess had to duck to keep her hat from hitting the doorway. Her dress was so wide, it brushed against the walls.

When they reached the door that led into the stables, Clover said, "Here are our unicorns. Are you looking for a particular type?"

"How about that one!" the princess said, pointing to Moondrop's stall.

"Oh, I don't think I should adopt Moondrop out yet. He just came in and is quite, um, weak."

"Weak? Oh, my dear, I have plenty of food in my castle perfect for making unicorns strong."

She is *plump*, thought Clover. *If she adopted Moondrop, maybe she'd feed him lots.*

The princess pulled out a twisted carrot from her purse and thrust it toward the unicorn. Moondrop snorted softly and backed away.

"A yummy, nummy carrot, darling unicorn."

"His name is Moondrop," said Clover.

"He has such a beautiful mane and tail. I just loooove gorgeous hair. I want to get to know him better," said the princess. "Leave. I'll summon you when I need you."

"Um . . . I don't think that's how we do things here. I have to stay with you. Why don't I show you some of the other unicorns too?" said Clover, biting her lip.

Then, all of a sudden, the bell in the front room rang again.

"Another customer," said Clover. "I can't believe it."

"It's your lucky day," said the princess.

"But I'm usually unlucky," said Clover.

The princess tilted her head. "You are?"

"I can't help it. I was born under a whisker-thin moon," said Clover. "My parents tell me it isn't a bad omen, but why else would they name me Clover?"

The bell rang again. "Oh, go ahead. I won't move. You can trust me, dear."

Clover wasn't sure about that, but she said, "I'll be back in a moment," and hurried down the hall, with a brief backward glance at the princess, who was gently stroking Moondrop. *It* would *be lucky if a nice princess adopted Moondrop,* thought Clover. But she wasn't sure this princess was nice.

In the front room a very different set of customers stood waiting at the desk. The man was tall with a grizzled beard. He was wearing an oversized shirt and patched overalls. Clover thought he must be a woodsman. A little girl stood beside him, holding his hand. She was much younger than Clover. Like the woodsman, she was wearing an oversized shirt and overalls. Her hair fell over her eyes in tangles.

"Hi, Miss, this is the Animal Adoption Agency, isn't it?" asked the woodsman. "My daughter and I weren't sure."

"Yes, it is. I'm Clover."

"Oh, good," said the woodsman, relieved. "I'm Olaf, and this is my daughter. I've been promising Susie, here, a pet for a long time, and today is finally the day."

"I love animals," piped up the little girl excitedly. "We have a donkey, and chickens too."

Do they know it is a magical animal adoption agency? wondered Clover. They looked about as magical as she was.

Just as she was debating what she should do, the princess came rushing out, nearly knocking Clover over.

"Your unicorns are not for me," said the princess.

"B-but . . ." Clover stammered.

The princess didn't utter another word as she swept past Clover. She no longer wore the pink gloves and was obviously trying to hide her hands as she hurried out, but Clover got a glimpse of them. Instead of being smooth and lovely like Clover imagined a princess's hands would be, they were wrinkly, with long, bony fingers and cracked, yellowed nails.

The princess clutched her purse tightly. From one corner of it hung something that made Clover's blood turn cold.

Hair.

But not just any hair—long and silvery and shiny hair.

Unicorn hair!

"Stop! Stop!" cried Clover.

The princess did not. She ran past the woodsman and his daughter, who looked stunned.

"STOP!" Clover yelled again, running after her.

The princess bolted out the door. Her pointy hat hit the top of the door frame and tumbled off her head.

She stooped to pick it up. Clover saw her face without its veil.

Her lips were pale and thin, and her eyes were cold and black. She was wearing earrings that looked like slivers of a broken mirror. Three thin white scars ran down her left cheek. Despite the scars, she was beautiful . . . in a terrifying way.

"Surprised, my dear?" she cackled. "I'd go check on your animals, if I were you." And with that, she grabbed her hat, turned, and was gone.

Clover's heart pounded. *Moondrop!* She spun around and ran across the entry room and through the door in a desperate dash to reach the unicorn. She sprinted down the hall to the stables.

Moondrop was neighing and rearing up on his hind legs in his stall, slashing his small rounded horn through the air. He kicked again and again at the stall door with his front hooves until finally it broke and fell to the side.

He ran out, his mane flying about his head like a flag in a storm. But his beautiful long tail . . .

It was ruined! Just half remained, all ragged, as though it had been hacked off with a dull knife.

"Moondrop! Stop! Stop!" The unicorn pushed past Clover and reared up. Clover shouted again. But her shouting further agitated the creature, and he continued to rear. One of his hooves glanced off Clover's foot.

She cried and fell back, her foot throbbing.

"Hush, hush," a voice whispered beside her. "Good horsey. Easy, there." Susie had followed Clover.

The little girl's tone was calm and steady. "Easy, easy. You're okay." She approached Moondrop cautiously. Moondrop froze.

When Susie reached Moondrop, she began to pet his neck in slow strokes, and then his forehead. His head fell gradually below his knees. Clover barely felt the pain in her foot, she was so amazed at the girl's effect on the injured unicorn. Within moments, Moondrop lay down, with the tiny girl crouching beside him, singing softly, *"Dreamy dust for you, sleepy dust for me, in this magic world, happy we shall be."*

"Wow," whispered Clover. "Thank you so much. How did you know how to do that?"

"Our donkey gets spooked easily too," she said,

continuing to stroke Moondrop's neck. "All you've got to do is keep your voice calm." She looked down at Moondrop's tail. "Did that mean woman do that?"

"She must have," said Clover. "I don't know why. She said she was a princess wanting to adopt a unicorn, but she seemed more like a witch or something like that."

"These unicorns are for adoption?" gasped Susie in awe.

Clover nodded just as Olaf entered the stables.

His hair was wild and he was huffing heavily. "I couldn't catch her," he said. "Tried to, but she got away through the Woods. What did she do?"

Clover and his daughter showed him the stub of Moondrop's tail.

"What would a witch want with a unicorn's tail?"

"I don't know. So she *is* a witch?" asked Clover.

"Looked like that to me," answered Olaf. "And a bad one at that. Only bad ones would take unicorn tails."

"Poor Moondrop. He's already been through a lot. The last princess who owned him treated him horribly."

"He likes my Susie, though," said the woodsman with a smile.

Indeed, Moondrop's head was now in Susie's lap.

"You were looking for a new pet. What do you think

about a unicorn, Susie?" asked her father.

"I can't have him. Unicorns are only princesses' pets, aren't they?" said Susie. "I'm not a princess." She brushed her matted bangs away from her face as if to prove the point.

But her father responded at once, "You are a princess. To me."

Clover nodded. She didn't care if Susie wasn't a princess. And she didn't think Mr. Jams would either. Mr. Jams had said just that a customer had to be "right"—he never said anything about unicorns needing to go to princesses only. In fact, he'd probably prefer that they didn't. But Moondrop was recovering. . . . Should she really let him go?

Susie was still stroking Moondrop's mane. A soft rumbling came from Moondrop's nostrils, the sound a cat might make when it's happy, and Clover knew. Susie was the right match. Her heart told her that with Susie, Moondrop would soon grow healthy and strong.

"You are perfect for Moondrop," she said aloud.

"Really?" said Susie.

"Really."

Clover found the adoption papers in the third drawer, just like Mr. Jams's note had said. She filled out the sections she needed to, including the date and the animal's name and description, and copied the special feeding instructions from the file. The only thing to write with was the fancy feather pen, but when she tried to use it, she splattered ink on her dress twice, to her embarrassment. So she took a regular pen from her pocket instead. *This is the sort of thing that Mom and Dad do all day long,* she thought. *Thank goodness it's only a small part of my job.*

While the woodsman and Susie filled out the rest of the papers, Clover went back to the stables and trimmed Moondrop's tail so at least it was even. In time it would grow out.

Her foot still throbbed, but only mildly now.

She looked at the stall gate. It was badly broken. Moondrop looked up and blinked.

"It's okay," said Clover. "It isn't your fault. It's mine. I let that witch into your stall." She hugged his neck. "It's my bad luck that brought that horrid witch who cut off your tail. I hope I never see her again."

Already Clover had encountered two witches, this one and the one who had pushed her into the puddle on her first day in the Woods. *Mr. Jams never should have left me in charge. At least he'll be back soon. The day after tomorrow. That's what his note said. Then everything will be fine.*

She felt a bit happier as she waved good-bye to Moondrop, Susie, and Olaf. Moondrop's tail, though very short, still swished nicely back and forth as he walked down the front path with Susie riding on his back.

7

Snort's Sneeze

That night Clover's parents noticed the key around her wrist. "It's for the Agency," she explained.

"Such responsibility already," said her mom.

"Well done, Clover," said her dad.

If only they knew the full truth of it! But Clover wasn't sure her parents would like to know that she was looking after the place all by herself, so she just nodded and smiled when her mom gave her a second helping of strawberries and ice cream. Ice cream, she decided, was good for melting away memories of mean witches.

But the memories returned in the morning, especially when a boy and his parents, a witch and a wizard, came into the Agency looking for a pet for the boy. At first, Clover didn't know what to think of the witch and wizard—were they bad or good? But they didn't seem too different from normal parents, except for their pointy hats and long black robes. They left empty-handed, debating between the toad and a salamander. They promised to return when they had made a decision.

Afterward, Clover took a postcard out of her bag. Her mom had given it to her before she left. It was from Emma.

On the front was a picture of a pony standing in a windswept field. On the back, Emma had written:

Hi Clover,

My pony's name is Gracie, and she's chestnut-colored. She's so cute! We have to sleep in bunk beds, and my bunkmate snores louder than a dragon! I wish you were here. Miss you!
                                        –XOXO, Emma

Clover smiled. Little did Emma know that Clover knew exactly how loudly a dragon snored now! Or, at least, a small dragon like Snort.

She took out a piece of blank paper from the desk. She wanted to tell Emma everything, but she couldn't tell her *anything*. Instead she wrote:

Hi Emma,

    Guess what? I got a job volunteering with animals. So far only a few unlucky things have happened to me. I miss you too!

                        –XOXO, Clover

Then Clover decided to add something special to it. There was still lots of room at the bottom of the page. In the stables, she stood by Coco's pen and sketched a picture of the unicorn. Coco was especially pretty. Close up, Clover saw there was a slight cinnamon tinge to Coco's horn and mane, which she hadn't noticed before. She tried to get Coco just right, with the sparkle in her eye and the exact length of horn. Emma would love it, and never imagine that Clover had sketched it from a REAL unicorn. Underneath she wrote, *I thought you might like this. I've been dreaming of unicorns lately. Send me a drawing of Gracie.*

After finishing her letter and tucking it in her bag to

mail, Clover had time to do a few things she had been longing to try.

During lunch, she cut up a bit of her apple and fed it to the fairy horses. They gathered around it, munching and swishing their paintbrush-sized tails. Then she brushed the coats of the unicorns until their hair shone like silver.

Later, after giving Esmeralda her vitamin pill—which took three attempts and involved lots of slimy toad spit—she played with the big toad. She placed Esmeralda on different-colored slips of paper to see if her warts would change color depending on her surroundings. They didn't. All Esmeralda did was snap her tongue and blink her bulging eyes.

Just as she was putting Esmeralda back in her tank,

the toad, with a grumpy croak, bounded out of her hands and hopped through the door and down the hall,

into the front room. It took a long time to capture her from under one of the chairs. When Clover finally did, the toad's warts were flashing all the colors of the rainbow, and Clover's heart was pounding too.

Just my luck to almost lose her, thought Clover. *What would I have told Mr. Jams? I'd better not play anymore.*

As soon as Clover placed Esmeralda back in her tank, the toad hopped to her favorite spot on the glass ball. Her warts stopped flashing and turned a pale green. *Hmm, I wonder if she changes color depending on her mood,* mused Clover. But she didn't want to take out the toad again and test her theory.

So she sank into the couch and read the Wish Book to see what other sorts of magical animals people longed for.

Each page was divided into three columns. On the far left was a column for the name, address, and phone number of the person who was requesting the animal; the middle column was for the animal; and the far-right

column was to check off if the
wish had been fulfilled.

The book was fascinating.

There was a woman who was looking
for a griffin to guard her chickens (check
mark). A mermaid princess looking for her lost hippocampus (sadly, no check mark). And below that, a dwarf
looking for a hippogriff (no check mark again). *I wonder what a hippogriff is*, thought Clover. Mr. Jams had
explained a hippocampus but not a hippogriff. *I'd better start a list of questions for Mr. Jams to ask him when
he returns.* Clover didn't have time to read through the
whole book and planned to continue the next day.

She closed the Agency with relief, knowing Mr. Jams
would be back tomorrow. And that night at home, she
slept as soundly as a salamander, without any dreams
at all.

♣

The next day, earlier than ever before, she hurried to
the Agency, hoping Mr. Jams was already there. She
imagined the lights on and the smell of cinnamon toast
and coffee filling the rooms.

But it was not to be. The Agency was dark and quiet.

Clover was jumpy all morning, expecting Mr. Jams to arrive at any moment. She spilled some of the unicorns' breakfast mush while she was pouring it into the buckets, but it wasn't as bad as spilling the oats, and it only took half the time to clean up.

She had just finished lunch, a cheese-and-mustard sandwich that her mom had packed for her, when the bell rang. She hurried to the entry, hoping it was Mr. Jams. But it wasn't.

Four people stood in the front room.

Three she recognized from the day before—the mother and father and their son, who today was dressed in red overalls and a red hat.

A fourth man, also a wizard (she could tell from his hat and robe), but much older, accompanied them. A wild red beard grew down past his stomach, and his spectacles made his eyes as large as an owl's. His cloak was decorated in red flames.

"We want to look at the salamander one more time," said the mother in a no-nonsense tone. "Isn't that right, Henry? They like fire just like you."

"I don't *like* fire, I like to fight—" started Henry.

"The toad is nice too," interrupted the boy's father.

"But, Dad, I don't want—"

"Toad or salamander, son. We already talked about this."

To break up the argument, Clover said, "And you brought another member of the family?"

The mother, father, and boy stared at the older wizard and shook their heads.

"We don't know him," said the boy.

"And I most certainly do not know them," replied the older wizard, whose voice was gruff and grumpy. "I am here for me dragon."

That declaration got everyone's attention.

"Your dragon?" quizzed Clover.

"Me dragon. He's black and ashy and not too old. Had 'im since he was an egg, and I want 'im back. I heard from a friend that you have 'im."

"Mr. Jams told me the dragon was abandoned here."

"More 'n likely he just wandered by," claimed the old wizard. "And you took 'im in. I don't know how he escaped, but I miss 'im. Miss his fire. Miss his claws. Miss his company."

Clover could hardly believe it. Snort hadn't been abandoned after all. This wizard looked like a dragon-keeping sort, with his wild red beard and the flames on his cloak.

"See, son?" said the boy's father. "That's what having

a pet is all about. It is about companionship. It's more than just training to be a good wizard, it's training to be a good person too."

"But I don't want to be a good wizard. I want to be a good firefighter. And I want a Dalmatian, not a toad or a salamander," cried the boy, stomping his foot.

"Hush!" said his mother.

They argued just like an ordinary family. "If you don't mind waiting, while I help Mr. . . . ?" Clover began.

"Sir Wickity," said the wizard.

"Sir Wickity," repeated Clover.

"Very well," said the boy's mother.

"Congratulations," the boy's father said to Sir Wickity. "It must be a fine feeling to have found a lost pet."

Clover couldn't help but think of Penny, flying somewhere in the Woods. She hoped her bird was safe and happy.

"Indeed," said Sir Wickity.

Clover got out Snort's paperwork. "This is Snort's file."

"Snort?" The wizard looked confused.

"Oh, you probably don't know him by that name. That's what we call the dragon. What's his real name?"

"Why . . . Ruffles, of course."

"Ruffles?"

"Named 'im after me pet owl, long gone now, poor thing."

Clover didn't think Ruffles was an appropriate name for Snort at all, or an owl either, for that matter, but she was too polite to say so. Sir Wickity sat down and she gave him the paperwork.

"Even though he was yours before, I need you to fill out these forms," said Clover. "I'll go get Snort. I just fed him, so he might be sleeping."

She went to the stables, stopping in the tack room for Snort's leash. The tack room was filled with weirdly shaped saddles and bridles of different sizes, from as tiny as an acorn, to larger than Clover's body. There was a whole wall of unicorn bridles, each on a separately labeled peg. There was a wall of leashes too. One leash had three giant collars attached to a single rope, which Clover deduced—somewhat alarmed—was probably for a creature with three heads. But she couldn't figure out what the bottles might be for. Several bottles were stacked in a dark corner, and whatever was in them twinkled brightly. When she peered closer, she read on a tag: *Stardust. Real* stardust? She added it to the list in her head of things to ask Mr. Jams.

She found Snort's leash, a thick chain one, on a peg with his name. It was heavy, with a clip at the end to attach to his collar.

As she guessed, Snort was asleep in his pen. Two thin tendrils of smoke spiraled up from his nostrils. He didn't look like a Ruffles at all. *What strange names magical people give to their pets*, thought Clover, remembering Mistypoo.

"Ruffles!" she called out, opening his door. "Ruffles!"

Snort didn't twitch, not even his tail.

"Snort!"

He woke up at once.

This made Clover a bit suspicious. *Maybe he is just more used to Snort now*, she thought. "Come on," she said. "Your owner, Sir Wickity, is here for you." Snort gave her a blank stare. He thumped his tail hard on the ground, and his nostrils flared.

Clover gulped. He didn't look very calm.

Nervously, she stepped into the pen, with the chain leash in one hand and a bucket of water in the other. Although she had fed him a few times now, each time she had made sure he was sleeping before she entered his pen and filled his bowl. She hadn't come too close, afraid he might snort fire.

Make sure he's nice and calm, Mr. Jams had said.

Clover remembered Susie and how she had calmed Moondrop. "Hush, hush," Clover whispered like Susie had. "Good Snort. Easy, Snort."

Snort's tail slowly stopped thumping. His snout twitched. Clover drew closer and closer. Finally she reached the little black dragon. His snout was resting on his front legs. Clover put down the pail and reached out a tentative hand. The dragon sniffled and her heart leapt, but he didn't breathe fire. Slowly Clover touched his back. His scales were smooth and slick, like ice. She began to quietly sing the song that Susie had sung, *"Dreamy dust for you, sleepy dust for me, in this magic world, happy we shall be."*

Snort's tail twitched in time to the tune. When Clover was done, he gazed up at her with his emerald eyes: they were big and hopeful, but worried-looking. They reminded Clover of her own. Her heart filled with ache for the dragon. He knew that he was trouble.

"Sweet dragon," Clover said. "We all have problems, you know. You shouldn't feel bad. You can't help it that you breathe fire."

Snort sniffled again, and although Clover's heart jumped, she didn't move her hand from his back.

She clipped the chain onto his metal collar. Snort stayed still and patient.

Clover led Snort out of his pen and down the hall, still wondering why he hadn't responded to "Ruffles." Before letting him go, she decided she would double-check to make sure that Snort really was Ruffles. How exactly she would do this, she wasn't sure.

Back in the front room, Henry and his family were waiting in the corner (still arguing), and Sir Wickity was sitting on the couch, writing. He stopped when Clover and Snort entered, and stood up.

"Aha! Me dragon," he said. "You have grown so big. You barely fit through the door. Look at your wings, your claws! They are so long."

Snort took a few steps toward the wizard, thumping his tail on the floor, breathing heavily. It seemed as if Snort did know Sir Wickity after all. Clover breathed a sigh of relief.

"Good draggie. That's me draggie," said Sir Wickity.

But Snort's breathing grew heavier and heavier as Sir Wickity spoke. His wings raised, as though he were afraid, and then . . .

Roar!

Snort let out a big flame.

It whooshed across the table covered in the adoption papers.

The papers burst into flames.

"Oh!" cried Clover, dropping the leash.

Sir Wickity jumped away from the burning papers and table, toward Snort.

"Fire!" cried Henry's mother.

"Stay back," commanded Henry's father.

Henry didn't listen. He stepped forward and pulled a wand from his pocket. He muttered under his breath and waved his wand in circles.

"I've got to get a bucket of water!" Clover exclaimed, mad at herself for not bringing one to begin with. She turned to go, when suddenly a bucket thumped down right in front of Henry.

"WOW!" Henry looked delighted. "It worked!"

He didn't waste any time. Dropping his wand, he grabbed the bucket with both hands and tossed the water over the table.

The water splashed in a wave over the papers, putting out the blaze.

Clover glanced over at Sir Wickity just in time to see him pull out *his* wand! Sir Wickity waved the wand across Snort's snout and said, *"Sleep, sleep, fall into a heap!"* Snort closed his eyes and sank to the floor. In a flash, Sir Wickity pulled out a pair of curved scissors from his cloak. With them, he clipped off Snort's longest talon. *Snap!* The talon made the sound of a stick breaking. Snort grunted, but he did not wake up. Sir Wickity stuffed the clippers, claw, and wand into his cloak pocket.

"What are you doing?" Clover cried. She noticed something else too. "Your beard is smoking!"

"FIRE!" yelled Sir Wickity in a much higher voice than before.

Then he did something very odd. He didn't try to smother the flames. Instead, he ripped the beard completely off his face, revealing three thin white scars.

He was no wizard. . . .

It was that witch again!

"YOU!" exclaimed Clover.

Henry's parents drew their wands.

"So long, unlucky little girl," the witch crowed as she fled out the door and disappeared, before Henry's parents had time to do anything.

Henry stomped on the beard, putting out the flame. When the fire was completely out, he ordered, "Open the windows and the doors," and started to do so himself.

As soon as the windows were open, cool air rushed into the room. The smoke cleared. Water dripped off the burnt table and trickled across the floor in a tiny stream.

Snort lay perfectly still beside the rug. His left foot was stretched outward, his third talon clipped close to his toe. While Henry's parents used magic to dry the table and rug, Clover hurried to his side, her shoes squishing with water. Thin tendrils of smoke rose from Snort's nostrils. At least he was breathing.

"He was put under a sleep spell," said Henry's father,

gently prodding one of Snort's wings. "He'll wake up soon enough. Sleep spells always wear off. But, tell us, what is this all about?"

Clover explained, as best she could, "That same witch tricked me yesterday and stole the hair from a unicorn's tail. And now she's tricked me again and stolen Snort's claw. I don't understand either. Why would a witch want a claw from a dragon?"

"I don't know," said Henry's father. "I don't know of any good spells that call for dragon claws. Dragon spit, yes, but dragon claws . . ."

"Will it grow back?"

"Dragons' claws always do, but very slowly," said Henry's father. "Much slower than our toenails."

Henry was crouching near Snort, watching the smoke spiral from his nostrils. "I never realized dragons were so amazing," he said, lightly touching Snort's scales.

"Careful, son. We don't know exactly how long that witch's sleep spell will last."

"If the witch can cast sleep spells, why doesn't she cast a spell on all of us and just come and get what she wants?" asked Clover.

"It is strange," said Henry's mother. "Usually wicked witches swoop in from far away, do something dreadful, then speed away in the dead of night. I wonder what she's up to."

"Well, at least the fire's out," said Clover. "Thanks to you, Henry."

"Yes, well done, son," said his father. "Water spells are extremely tricky. Your mother's water spells cause floods, and mine tend to end with lightning."

"Thanks. I made it up myself," said Henry, looking proud. "I have other water spells too—depending on the type of fire. Firefighters must be on guard at all times."

"You'd be the perfect owner for Snort," said Clover. "He's always lighting things on fire."

The boy's eyes went big. "I never thought about it like that, but you're right. He needs someone like me."

"A dragon?" His mother shook her head. "That's a much bigger pet than we talked about."

"Wizards don't have dragons as pets, son. Toads, salamanders, owls . . ." said his father.

"Please can I adopt him? You said it wasn't just about learning to be a wizard. It was also about learning to be a good person."

"You did say that," his mother said to his father.

"I did, didn't I?" said his father with a sigh.

♣

By the time new paperwork was made up and filled out, and Clover had found the pamphlets on dragon care for Henry, including one titled *Your Dragon's First Flight and Beyond*, Snort had awoken. He rose and walked toward Clover with a bit of a hobble, his tail dragging on the floor. Suddenly, Clover's heart felt like it was dragging too. Snort was tricky to deal with, but he was also the first dragon she had known. Mr. Jams cared about him a lot too. Would Mr. Jams mind that she had let him go? Then she remembered Mr. Jams's words—*Adoption is our Agency's purpose*—and felt better.

Henry would take care of Snort. Snort would finally have a family, a friend—a home.

"Good Snort," said Clover, clipping his leash back on. "Look, you have a new owner."

Snort thumped his tail on the ground and looked from her to Henry.

"Don't worry, Snort. What happened with that bad witch won't happen again. This is a nice wizard. He will make sure you're happy."

Henry smiled. "That's right," he said. He pulled out gloves from his pockets. "Firefighter's fireproof gloves," he explained. "I have a lot of stuff that'll be good for taking care of Snort."

"You're going to keep his name the same?"

"Yeah, of course." Henry put on the gloves and rubbed Snort's nose gently. Snort let out a yawn.

Soon Snort, a very happy Henry, and his rather skeptical parents were on their way. It was the end of the day. And Mr. Jams still wasn't back.

Clover frowned. *Where can he be?*

♣

After feeding the animals, but before locking up, Clover dried her shoes by putting them on top of the salamander tank. While she waited, she played with the fairy horses, letting them gallop around her palms. Their tiny hooves made Clover's skin tingle. Tansy seemed to like her the best, and Clover had to use a sugar cube to coax the little horse to leave her hand. Secretly, Clover hoped she wouldn't get adopted soon.

When she put on her shoes they were toasty warm.

I won't let that witch trick me again, thought Clover, turning off the lights.

But she was worried that her bad luck had other plans.

8

Esmeralda's Enchantment

Clover got up early again, skipping breakfast this time but promising her parents she'd eat at the Agency. She had a present to give to the gnome and she hoped he'd like it. But more than that, she was anxious to find out if Mr. Jams was back.

But the moment she started up the curved path, her heart sank. All the lights at the Agency were off. The garden gnome stood awake and alert at the front gate.

After finishing the morning feeding and grooming, Clover took the rug outside and beat it to get rid of ashes. She put it back, then went to check on the gnome, who was now fast asleep in the sun.

"Hi," she said, trying to strike up a conversation.

He opened one eye a sliver.

"I wish Mr. Jams had left a number for me to call or something. Do you think he's okay?"

The gnome said nothing. But his forehead creased.

"Sorry. I didn't mean to upset you," said Clover. "It's just that he said he would be back yesterday."

The lines on the gnome's forehead grew deeper.

"You're doing a great job," added Clover quickly. "Nothing's gone wrong at night. In fact . . ." She took her tortoise paperweight out of her pocket. "I brought this for you. I thought you might like it. It's made of jade. Jade's supposed to be lucky, you know."

The gnome's forehead relaxed and he closed his eye. The tips of his white mustache rose up a bit. Clover placed the gift beside the gnome's boots. The tortoise, the same shade of dark green as the grass, became almost invisible.

With a brief glance past the gate into the mysterious Woods, Clover went back inside. Her heart was heavy like the paperweight. "I need a distraction," she said out loud.

She remembered Mr. Jams had told her to help herself to cinnamon toast. And all this worrying had made her hungry, and she *had* skipped breakfast, after all. She opened Mr. Jams's special cupboard full of sugar and cinnamon, butter and bread. Even after three days, the bread seemed remarkably fresh. The first slice burned in the toaster. But she popped the next slice up early and got it right. As she buttered the golden toast and sprinkled on the cinnamon and sugar, Clover remembered the Wish Book.

I'll finish reading it, she thought. Then she had an idea. Maybe the witch had put in a request for animals before and it was recorded in the Wish Book. Maybe she could find out something more about her. Of course, she knew it was unlikely, especially since it seemed the witch just came in and stole what she wanted, but it was worth looking into.

With her snack in one hand and the book in the other, Clover curled up on the couch and opened the pages to where she had left off.

A tooth fairy looking for a toothless night-light bug (check mark). A troll looking for a hippogriff (no check mark). A fairy godmother seeking a coach mouse (no check mark). A prince looking for a peryton (no check mark).

There sure were a lot of animals she had never heard of before. She added them to her list of things to ask

Mr. Jams. There were many more entries that weren't checked off. But no witches.

She flipped the page, munching the last bit of her toast, scanning only for the entries that hadn't been checked and for witches. A jockey looking for a winged horse. A professor looking for a sphinx. A giant looking for a three-headed dog. "Oh, that's what the leash with the three collars is for!" exclaimed Clover.

She flipped to the next page. A wizard looking for a phoenix. A pixie looking for a starbird. Still no witches.

And then she noticed a wish that made her pause.

It was written very neatly at the bottom of a page: *Miss Opal, fortune-teller, 22 Sibyl Lane, 222-222-SEER / Looking for a mood creature, firefly preferred, but any type will do.*

There was no check mark in the right-hand column.

"Mood creature?" wondered Clover. Although she had never heard of a mood creature, she immediately thought of Esmeralda, and how the toad's colors changed when she was excited. Esmeralda was cursed, Mr. Jams had said. But even so, it looked like the curse was there to stay. So maybe the toad was a mood creature now!

A toad wasn't exactly a firefly, but still . . .

What should she do? Should she call Miss Opal? But where was the phone?

In all her time at the Agency, she had never heard the phone ring.

She got up and searched the room.

At last she spied it, perched on top of the bookshelf. It was an ancient thing, with a dial and a single receiver at the end of a twisty cord. She had to stand on a chair to reach it.

She could feel something else on top of the bookshelf, too. She stood on her tiptoes and could just see, lying behind the phone, a big sword in a leather sheath. The initials *T.J.* were inscribed on the handle.

I wonder where Mr. Jams got that, thought Clover, remembering the dark look he had given her when he spoke about knights. Careful to avoid the dusty sword, she picked up the phone and carried it to the desk. The twisty cord stretched out like a noodle.

She dialed Miss Opal's number. The phone rang on the other end a few times, and then a voice answered.

"Miss Opal, your friendly fortune-teller, here. What can I see for you?"

"Well, I'm calling from the M.A.A.A.—" Clover started.

Miss Opal interrupted, "Oh, you must be Clover."

Clover jumped. *Wow, she must be a good fortune-teller!*

"Go on. . . ." said Miss Opal.

"Well, I was phoning because . . . because I was reading through the Wish Book, and I noticed your wish. I think we have a pet here that might be a fit for you."

"A mood creature? A firefly?"

"Yes, possibly a mood creature, but she's not a firefly. She's a toad."

"A toad?" Miss Opal seemed puzzled. Then, as though she had realized something suddenly, she exclaimed, "A TOAD!"

There was a sharp click as Miss Opal hung up.

Clover put down the receiver with a sigh. *I guess she*

didn't want a toad. It had been a silly idea to call. But she *had* distracted herself from thinking of what had happened to Mr. Jams—at least for a few moments.

She put away the Wish Book, cleaned up her plate, and fed the animals their lunches. She had just finished feeding Esmeralda, this time hiding the vitamin pill in a squashed fly, when the bell at the front rang. She hurried to see who it was.

An ordinary-looking lady in a pretty, yet plain, sweater and jeans and flats stood at the front desk. A thin golden chain hung around her neck. Her white hair was swept back in a ponytail. She looked a little like Clover's mom, but might be as old as her grandma. It was impossible to tell.

"How may I help you?" asked Clover hesitantly. She didn't want to be tricked by that witch again. But unless the witch had shape-shifted, there was no way this lady was her. Clover could tell she wasn't wearing makeup and, although there were a few wrinkles around her eyes, her skin was rosy and free of any blemishes, much less scars.

"I'm Miss Opal," the lady said.

"Miss Opal?" Clover blanched. *This lady* was the fortune-teller?

This was NOT at all how Clover pictured the fortune-teller. Fortune-tellers, at least the ones that she had read about, wore ropes of beads and rainbow-colored dresses and smelled of exotic perfumes.

"You must be Clover. I'm friends with Olaf, the woods-man. He and Susie live near me. They told me about you and how you helped them with Susie's unicorn."

"Oh, *that's* how you knew my name," said Clover.

Miss Opal laughed. "Of course. Now, please, I would like to see the toad you mentioned."

"Yes," said Clover, with a smile. "I know it's not quite the same as a firefly, but I hope you like Esmeralda."

She led Miss Opal down the hall and into the first room. But when they reached Esmeralda's tank, it was empty!

"Oh no!" cried Clover. The lid of the tank was partially open. "I just finished feeding her. But I thought I put the lid back on. In fact, I checked it. I'm sure."

"Maybe she jumped and pushed it off?" suggested Miss Opal.

Clover puzzled. "Maybe. Perhaps the vitamin pills are making her stronger."

"Vitamin pills?" said Miss Opal. "Do toads need vitamin pills?"

"Esmeralda does," said Clover. "She was put under a curse that makes her change color. But I discovered that she changes color based on her mood. That's why I thought you would like her. But now she's lost! It's just my luck. . . ."

Clover bent down, searching for Esmeralda under the tables. "Esmeralda!" she called out. "Esmeralda!"

There was no movement, no sound. Not even one croak. "ESMERALDA!" She felt tears sting her eyes.

"Oh my dear," said Miss Opal, crouching beside Clover and patting her shoulder, "Not to worry. Here, let me."

Miss Opal took a breath and called, "FLIT! FLIT! Come here, Flit!"

"Flit?" said Clover, confused. "Why . . ."

But she didn't have a chance to finish. With a chorus of happy croaks, the toad appeared in the doorway, hopping straight toward Miss Opal. She was jumping very high (the vitamin pills, perhaps), and each time she hopped her warts changed from violet to blue and back again. She leapt into Miss Opal's hands.

"It IS you, Flit! Oh, Flit, I thought I'd never see you again!"

With that, the toad's warts turned as pink as bubble gum.

Miss Opal looked at Clover, whose mouth was hanging open. "I guess you are wondering what's going on?"

"Yes," said Clover, nodding vigorously.

"It's a long story. Perhaps we should get comfy."

♣

Clover made herself and Miss Opal slices of cinnamon toast as Miss Opal filled out the paperwork. After Clover checked it, they sat on the couch and Miss Opal told her story. Esmeralda—Flit—settled on Miss Opal's lap. Her warts were now a calm sea green.

Miss Opal closed her eyes. "Long, long ago now, when I was much younger—"

"You don't look *that* old," interrupted Clover.

Miss Opal blushed. "Well, I do have a few wrinkles now. We fortune-tellers are lucky to live long lives. But this story happens when I had just finished my training as a fortune-teller. My teacher gave me a mood creature to congratulate me. It was a pet firefly. Like you, many people think they change color depending on their own emotions. But actually mood creatures change based on the moods of people around them. And they can even predict a person's feelings in the future. Fortune-tellers

102

are able to tell which colors are foretelling a person's future feelings. That's why mood creatures are a great help to us."

Clover remembered how frantic she had felt when the toad had escaped, and how her warts had been flashing all the colors of the rainbow. It made sense.

"My firefly and I got along at once. I named her Flit. I didn't even need to keep Flit in a cage, she was that attached to me.

"Then, one day, something terrible happened. A witch and her wizard husband came to have their baby's fortune told. Instantly I saw that their child would bring great luck to others when she grew up. I thought they would be thrilled with the prophecy, but they were outraged. I didn't realize this witch and wizard were evil—they had hidden that well when they first arrived—and they wanted their child to carry on the wicked tradition of their families. They tried to curse me, but I dodged their spell. It hit Flit instead. I ran away to escape them, and when I came back, Flit was gone. I assumed she flew out one of the open doors or windows. I was heartbroken. I searched everywhere for my little firefly. I even checked here for her, but I didn't realize she had been turned into a toad. So many years have passed; I thought I would never see her again. Until you called today. It suddenly struck me that the witch's curse must have been to change me into a toad, but it hit Flit instead, and transformed her. Thanks to you, we've been reunited at last."

"Wow!" said Clover. "So she *is* cursed, but the curse doesn't make her change color. The curse made her a toad! How will you change her back?"

Miss Opal smiled at the warty lump on her lap. "I don't think I can. At least because she is bigger, it is easier to see her colors." Miss Opal turned her smile to Clover. "As part of my thanks, I'd like to offer you a free fortune."

Clover shook her head forcefully. "No thanks. I'd rather not know. Things don't usually work out well for me."

"Well, the offer stands, if you ever want to come by. I live in the Woods near Olaf and Susie. I must be on my way, then."

Clover gave Esmeralda—Flit—a kiss good-bye. Instantly Flit's warts shone in a mix of cinnamon and gold, just like the toast. "It looks like Flit gave you a fortune anyway," said Miss Opal.

"What do you mean?" asked Clover.

Miss Opal winked. "I thought you didn't want to know."

"You're right. I don't," said Clover, resolute.

"Few fortunes are bad, Clover," said Miss Opal. "Some, in fact, are good. Very good." With that, she gave Clover another wink. Holding her pet close to her chest, she headed out the door.

Clover shook her head, but secretly hoped Miss Opal's words were true.

She watched out the window as Miss Opal walked down the path. Miss Opal and the toad were perfect together. She felt a twinge of longing. And of missing. She knew she would miss Esmeralda. (She just couldn't get herself to say Flit.) She already missed Moondrop and Snort, even though she was happy for them too. It was a funny feeling—half happy, half sad. *I guess that comes with working at an adoption agency. That's what Mr. Jams meant about keeping an open but guarded heart.*

As she did her chores, she couldn't help but gaze at the empty pens in the stables and empty cages in the small animals' room. She hoped all the animals that had once lived there were doing well—the griffin and the winged horse, and the witch's little white kitten. She stood a long time in front of Snort's pen, the sad part of her heart growing bigger.

But later, as Clover put a check mark in the far-right column in the Wish Book, beside Miss Opal's entry, she felt more happy than sad. The day was ending, and that nasty witch hadn't turned up. Clover had made a successful match without anything going wrong. Even though Mr. Jams wasn't back, it felt like things were finally looking up.

9

A Wicked
Plan

The next morning, as Clover walked up the path, she heard a ringing coming from inside the Agency. It sounded like the phone!

It must *be Mr. Jams*, she thought, hurrying to unlock the front door. She rushed into the room.

"Hello?" she said, picking up the receiver. "Mr. Jams?"

"Mr. Jams?" a faint voice on the other end said at the same time.

"No. I'm not Mr. Jams," said Clover. "I'm a volunteer helping at the Agency. What can I do for you?"

"Oh, thank goodness!" croaked a woman's voice on the other end. The voice sounded desperate. "I . . . I was hoping to catch Mr. Jams, but if you are helping there, you will do. I was taking my morning stroll in the Woods when . . . oh goodness me . . . lo and behold, I saw a little white kitten stuck in a tree. She's still there. She looks very scared. I would climb the tree myself, but I am too old and weak. I hobbled home as fast as I could to phone Mr. Jams. Will you come and rescue her?"

"Well . . ." Clover hesitated. Mr. Jams hadn't told her what to do in this situation.

"Please hurry!" the lady continued. "I think I saw a witch!"

Clover shuddered. *A little white cat,* she thought. *It might be the one that was adopted from the Agency. It might be in danger from that witch.*

"Where is the tree?" she asked.

"Follow the path, past the Agency, into the Heart of the Woods. It's the old oak in the middle of the forest. You can't miss it. Oh goodness me, please hurry. I will meet you there."

"I'll come right away," said Clover. She hung up the phone, grabbed her coat and the rope ladder from the storage room, and rushed out the door, making sure to lock it behind her. She turned the ENTER sign to CLOSED (EVEN FOR ROYALTY!). She stopped for a few moments at the front gate to shake awake the gnome. He blinked at her groggily.

"I've got to go and rescue a cat," said Clover. "Protect the Agency while I'm gone, okay? I'll be back soon."

She hurried to the signposts and found the one that read HEART. She had yet to venture anywhere in the Woods except to the Agency. And now here she was, going into the very middle of it. Clover knew Mr. Jams said there were no beasties in the Woods, but the Heart of the Woods sounded like the sort of place scary creatures might live. Still, with a deep breath, she ran on.

The trees in this part of the Woods, crooked and bare, looked lifeless. No birds chattered. No squirrels scurried. She could understand why most people from her village stayed away from the Woods, at least this section. It *was* spooky. She sang the song that Susie had sung to Moondrop and she had sung to Snort, to keep herself calm: *"Dreamy dust for you, sleepy dust for me, in this magic world, happy we shall be."*

She had just noticed a ring of moon-colored mushrooms when a faint voice interrupted her thoughts. "Here—over here!"

It was the same feeble voice she had heard on the phone.

Clover looked up. There stood a giant tree. The leaves were broad and the bark thick and rough like a toad's skin.

She was sure it was the right oak tree.

But the old woman who had called out to her was nowhere to be seen. She peered up at the tree. She couldn't see anything at first except green leaves and brown branches, but then there was a flash of white. Clover rose up on her tiptoes, trying to spy more white. "Kitty? Is that you?"

Suddenly, a woman's face loomed down out of the leaves. A face with three scars!

"Sleep, sleep, fall into a heap!"

As soon as the spell was cast, everything went dark.

♣

When Clover awoke she was tied to a hard chair in a large room that smelled like onions and smoke. A squat pot hung over burning coals in the fireplace near her. On the mantel perched a stuffed crow. Spilled salt and pepper speckled the floor. A few open umbrellas lay in dusty corners. Pointed black-heeled shoes sat on a wooden table in the center of the room.

The table was also covered in a strange assortment of objects including a saltshaker, a broken horseshoe, a pile of two-leaf clovers, and, most awful of all . . . dead ladybugs, spiders, and bees. Beside the table, on a small, high stool, was a birdcage with a little white kitten, just a bit larger than a ball of yarn, locked inside. Clover was sure he was the same kitten she had seen days ago, when she'd gone to the Agency for the first time—but he looked much scruffier and thinner and sadder. His green eyes were dull and his tail limp.

"Well, well, our unlucky child has finally awoken," crowed a voice. The witch entered from a back room. She wasn't wearing a princess's veil this time, or a wizard's cloak, just a simple black dress. Her long dark hair fell in waves to her waist. She was wearing her broken-mirror earrings. "At last we properly meet. I am Ms. Wickity."

"Let me go!" cried Clover, struggling against the rope around her wrists that held her tight to the chair.

"And lose my final ingredient? Sorry, but you, my child, are too important. I have been searching for someone like you for a very long time. Now I can finish my potion." She strode over to Clover and stood so close Clover could smell her vile onion-and-garlic breath. "You know, my child, we share a common problem— luck. You are unlucky and I am supposed to be the opposite. When I was baby a fortune-teller prophesied that one day I would bring great luck to others, spreading good wherever I went."

Clover jolted, remembering the fortune-teller's story. "It was Miss Opal! Your parents turned her firefly into a toad."

"Miss Opal indeed!" spat Ms. Wickity. "That loathsome fortune-teller cursed me forever. When my potion is complete, she will be the first one I get."

"B-but . . . everyone wants luck," stammered Clover.

"Luck!" spat Ms. Wickity. "I come from a long line of wicked witches. Wicked witches cast bad luck upon people—not good luck. I grew up afraid to wave my own wand, in case I might make the prophecy come true. Eventually I realized there was only one thing to do: create a lifetime supply of bad-luck potion, so I can spread it around wherever I go. I have been trying to make the potion since I was very young. When I was only a witch in training, I pulled hair from a black cat for one of my attempts, and that is how I ended up with these scars. But some ingredients were impossible to obtain. I could never capture a wild dragon, and pet dragons are ridiculously expensive. I should have thought of looking for a magical animal adoption agency years ago. And imagine my delight to find YOU there as well!"

As she spoke, she popped the objects on the table one by one into the pot. When the tabletop was nearly cleared, she swept a handful of sparkly hairs off it, counted them out until she reached thirteen, then threw them into the pot too. They sizzled.

"Those are Moondrop's hairs!" cried Clover.

The witch smiled a twisted smile and took the last item off the table: a long green claw.

"And that's Snort's claw!"

The witch smiled again, then tossed it into the cauldron and watched the brew bubble. "At last, it is ready for the final and most challenging ingredient. The blood of an unlucky child. That's you, my dear."

"No!" cried Clover. She struggled once again to free her hands, pulling and tugging, but the ropes didn't give.

"There is no point in fighting. You know you are unlucky, and anything you do will simply worsen your situation." Ms. Wickity drew out her wand and pointed it at Clover. *"Free, free, stand by me."* The ropes magically fell from Clover's wrists and, as though someone was controlling her limbs, Clover jerked to her feet and whooshed next to Ms. Wickity, landing with such force she nearly tumbled into the pot.

Now untied, Clover knew this was her chance to escape, but before she could make a move, Ms. Wickity's cold, scaly fingers wrapped around her wrist like the coils of a snake. With her other hand, Ms. Wickity pulled a pin from her hat. Clover struggled, but Ms. Wickity held her fast, and jabbed the pin deep into Clover's thumb.

"Ouch!" yelled Clover.

"Silence!" snapped Ms. Wickity, stretching Clover's hand over the brew.

The steam scalded Clover's skin as Ms. Wickity squeezed three drops of blood into the pot.

The moment the last drop touched the potion, a green-and-white mist rose up. Ms. Wickity shoved Clover away, saying, *"Tie, tie, stay there till you die."* Clover flew back to the chair, powerless against the spell, and the rope twisted around her wrists, tighter than before.

Ms. Wickity removed the pot from over the fire and set it on the table. With a ladle she scooped some of the brew into a small spray bottle that looked like one of Clover's mother's perfume bottles, except it was made from glass as black as smoke.

"Now to test it. It's so powerful just one mist will change this pathetic white cat into an unlucky black one, truly wicked and fit for a witch."

"You're not going to use it on the kitten!" gasped Clover.

Ms. Wickity just laughed and put the nozzle of the bottle in through the bars of the cage and aimed it at the kitten's head.

The kitten mewed pitifully.

"You stupid little misfit. This will actually help you. Don't you want to be a proper witch's cat?"

The tiny kitten backed into the far corner of the cage.

Ms. Wickity sprayed a puff of the potion. The kitten sneezed . . . then froze. His tail stuck straight up in the air like an exclamation point.

Clover couldn't bear to watch.

She closed her eyes.

When she opened them again, she blinked in surprise.

The kitten wasn't white anymore.

But it wasn't black either.

The kitten had turned a beautiful green!

10

Serendipity

It was the loveliest color Clover had ever seen—the color of new grass, peas, peppermint leaves, and emeralds. The color of clovers.

The little kitten looked pleased and licked the green fur on the back of his paw.

"WHAT?" Ms. Wickity screeched. "Impossible!" She pointed her finger at Clover. "You told me you were unlucky, but green is the LUCKIEST of colors! You lied to me. You must be a LUCKY child."

"No! I'm not lucky!" said Clover.

Ms. Wickity spun around and threw open a cupboard, grabbing a recipe book to double-check her ingredients.

Meanwhile, Clover's mind was spinning. A LUCKY child? Her? Then she thought about it, and something remarkable occurred to her. . . .

If she HADN'T messed up with Ms. Wickity, Moondrop and Snort wouldn't have been adopted by Susie and Henry—and they were perfect matches.

If she HADN'T lost Penny, she would NEVER have come to the M.A.A.A. and met Moondrop and Snort and all the wonderful magical animals in the first place. And she would never have been able to help Mr. Jams so he could leave on his rescue mission (even if he hadn't come back yet), or have been able to help animals herself.

Maybe she wasn't so unlucky after all!

The kitten mewed.

Clover needed to rescue the kitten. The witch was still bent over her book, muttering and swearing to herself, but who knew what she might do next.

Clover pulled against the ropes again and felt something dig into her skin. The key! Around her wrist was the Agency key—carved from a tooth, with sharp teeth of its own. If she HADN'T tied the key around her wrist it wouldn't be here to help her now. And, amazingly, Ms. Wickity hadn't noticed it.

Suddenly, Clover felt powerful.

She felt lucky!

She struggled to grasp the key with her opposite hand. She twisted and wiggled until her grip grew firm, and then she scraped the key's sharp edge across the rope—back and forth, back and forth. At first, it seemed like nothing was happening, but then she felt one strand of the rope snap. She sawed furiously, thankful that the witch was absorbed in her book.

Just as Clover felt the last strand of the rope give, Ms. Wickity looked up at the kitten. "Maybe the cat just needs MORE potion. Yes, that has to be it. I'll spray the beast again!"

"Leave that kitten alone!" Clover yelled. She leapt out of the chair and grabbed the pot from the table, throwing its entire contents at the witch.

SPLASH!

Ms. Wickity shrieked and jumped back, but not quite in time. The potion splashed across her hands, drenching them. Instantly her fingers turned from crooked and bony to straight and beautiful. Her cracked, yellow nails became smooth and bright green. "My hands!" screeched Ms. Wickity. While the witch frantically wiped her hands on her cloak, Clover grabbed the cage with the kitten inside and hugged it close to her chest.

"You're not going anywhere!" Ms. Wickity pulled her wand from her pocket and pointed it at Clover. *"Sleep, sleep, fall into a heap!"*

Clover blinked. Instead of feeling sleepy, she felt exactly the opposite—awake and energetic. She hurried toward the door.

Ms. Wickity shouted another spell, pointing her wand at her broom: *"Tip, flip, make her trip!"*

But instead of the broom falling down and tripping Clover, it fell onto the handle of the door and pushed it open.

Something was really wrong with Ms. Wickity's spells.

Ms. Wickity's eyes went wide with horror as she cried out another one, *"Bam, bam, door slam!"*

A whoosh of wind escaped from the witch's wand, and pushed the door farther open instead.

"That potion!" shrieked Ms. Wickity, her face now furious red. "It's making me cast lucky spells! The terrible prophecy has come true!"

Clover was off and running down the path. Ms. Wickity chased behind her, still crying out spells: *"Spike, spike, lightning strike!"* and *"Sting, sting, bees take wing!*" When Clover looked back, instead of lightning and bees, rainbows and butterflies were flying out of the open door.

♣

Clover ran the whole way back to the Agency, hugging the cage with the kitten in it. She glimpsed a yellow bird as she was running and wondered if it might be Penny, but she was afraid the witch was after her and didn't stop. She ran past the oak tree, past the ring of mushrooms. It wasn't long before she emerged into the clearing, panting and hot.

The Agency was just up ahead, crooked and moss-covered as ever. The sight of it filled Clover with happiness.

She hurried up the path that curved like a dragon's tail. When she reached the garden gnome, standing by the door with his arms crossed, she patted him on the head.

"Good job," she said.

With a grunt, the gnome fell asleep at once.

Clover unlocked the door and took a deep breath. The building still smelled very strongly of smoke, a

reminder of Snort. She could hear the unicorns neighing from the back. They were hungry.

Boy, do I have a lot of work to do, thought Clover.

First she freed the kitten from the cage. He leapt out happily and joined her as she fed the animals. They were so hungry, one of the unicorns even nibbled at her hair! Then she began to clean up the Agency. She found a hammer and nails in the storage room and fixed Moondrop's stall door. Every time she had used a hammer before she had hit her fingers, but this time she wasn't nervous. She confidently pounded away, and didn't strike herself once. She changed the hay in the unicorns' stables, and vigorously cleaned Moondrop's and Snort's pens so they were ready for new animals. She moved on to the front room. With a bucket and mop and an armful of rags, she scrubbed the floor, and dusted the tables and bookshelves. She beat the rug again, making sure it was as clean as it could be, and she put a vase of flowers over the burnt spot on the table. When she was done, the entire Agency sparkled.

Everything was in order. She even wrote out all her questions for Mr. Jams (like *What is a hippogriff?* and *What is the stardust for?*) so she wouldn't forget them. Then she put on the kettle and brewed a cup of green tea, in honor of the little kitten, and together she and the kitten curled up on the couch in the front room.

As she stroked the kitten and waited for the tea to cool, she thought about how strange it was that Ms. Wickity had made her own fortune come true. Clover almost felt sorry for the witch; but then the kitten purred in her lap, and she was so glad that the awful witch never would, never COULD, do harm again.

In the last few days, so much had changed. Her friendless, luckless summer had transformed into one filled with enchantment and excitement. Just days ago, she hadn't been certain magic existed. Now she knew it did. It was her bad luck that she didn't believe in anymore.

Things happened. Bad things. Good things. It was what you did with them that mattered. And so far, Clover was proud of what she had done. She was proud of all the matches she had made, proud of keeping the Agency safe, proud of saving the kitten. Those were lucky happenings of her own making.

Although she could never share these things with her parents, she knew they would be extra proud of her. Her mom was right—being plucky *had* made her lucky.

Dipping a spoonful of honey into her tea, she had an idea.

"I'll call you Dipity," Clover announced to the kitten. "Short for 'Serendipity,' which means 'lucky happenings.' That's a good name for you."

The kitten flicked his green tail in approval.

She hoped Mr. Jams would let her keep him.

And just as she thought of Mr. Jams, she heard the front door creak open and Mr. Jams's voice: "Clover, I've returned!"

He pushed through the door. Dipity leapt off Clover's lap and hid under the couch.

Mr. Jams's pointed beard was tangled with bits of twigs, and one knee of his pants was ripped. His boots were covered in muck and his jacket was torn and stained. But his blue eyes twinkled with excitement. He smiled as he glanced at the room. "Very neat and calm in here, I must say. Not a horse feather out of place. Nothing much happened, then? No problems? I'm sorry I am a little late. There was no way around it. But I knew you could handle it. I'm lucky you were here to help."

127

"Well . . ." started Clover. "There were a *few* things that happened."

"And I can't wait to hear about them. But first, no time to delay. Come outside—I need your help bringing it in."

"*It?* What is it? What animal did you rescue?"

"It's not really an animal. At least not yet. But it will be. Beaks and eggshells, will it ever."

"What do you mean?" Clover's heart started to pound with excitement.

But Mr. Jams had already turned around and hurried out the door.

As Clover hurried after him, she realized she was walking with a bounce in her step. This time, she didn't change it.

ACKNOWLEDGMENTS

To a large degree, I believe, like Clover does at the end of this book, that you make your own luck. But when it comes to all the people who helped me bring this book to life, I have been completely and totally lucky beyond my own making. Thank you to all those people: my dad, who is Mr. Jams; my mom and my family; my writing soul mate, Vikki Vansickle; my writing group, the Inkslingers—Rachelle Delaney, Tanya Lloyd Kyi, Lori Sherritt-Fleming, Maryn Quarless, Shannon Ozirny, and Christy Goerzen; Lee Edward Fodi, who was there when this story was born; Dimiter Savoff, for believing in my writing; my writing friends James and KC, and the whole Storm Crow gang; my wonderful

Disney • Hyperion team, especially Stephanie Lurie, editors Catherine Onder and Rotem Moscovich, editorial assistant Julie Moody, and designers Sara Gillingham and Joann Hill; my wonderful HarperCollins Canada team, especially editor Hadley Dyer; and the talented Alexandra Boiger. Special thanks to my amazing agent, Emily Van Beek; to my dear husband, Luke; and finally, most of all, to Tiffany Stone for her utterly thoughtful edits and ideas and time (and her whole family for putting up with Clover). Tiff, you are the best.

KALLIE GEORGE works as an author and editor in Vancouver, Canada, and she holds a master's degree in children's literature from the University of British Columbia. In addition to writing and editing, Kallie is a speaker and leads workshops for aspiring writers. She dreams of one day adopting a fairy horse. Visit her online at kalliegeorge.com.

ALEXANDRA BOIGER grew up in Munich, Germany, where she studied graphic design, and then began a career in feature animation, allowing her to work for Warner Bros. UK and DreamWorks. After transitioning to children's book illustration, she has worked on numerous popular titles, including the Tallulah series. She lives with her husband and daughter in northern California. See more of her work online at alexandraboiger.com.